A Silly Book for Allie
love Gma & Gpa

A Silly Book for Allie
love Gma & Gpa

Is Mommy?

words by
Victoria Chang
and
pictures by
Marla Frazee

Beach Lane Books
NEW YORK • LONDON • TORONTO • SYDNEY • NEW DELHI

To Penny and Winnie,
who love their mommy,
no matter what
—V. C.

To my mommy
and her mommy
and her mommy . . .
—M. F.

BEACH LANE BOOKS
An imprint of Simon & Schuster Children's Publishing Division
1230 Avenue of the Americas, New York, New York 10020
Text copyright © 2015 by Victoria Chang
Illustrations copyright © 2015 by Marla Frazee
BEACH LANE BOOKS is a trademark of Simon & Schuster, Inc.
For information about special discounts for bulk purchases, please
contact Simon & Schuster Special Sales at 1-866-506-1949 or
business@simonandschuster.com.
The Simon & Schuster Speakers Bureau can bring authors to your live
event. For more information or to book an event, contact the Simon
& Schuster Speakers Bureau at 1-866-248-3049 or visit our website at
www.simonspeakers.com.
Book design by Marla Frazee and Ann Bobco
The text for this book is set in Neutraface Text Bold in combination
with hand-lettering by Marla Frazee.
The illustrations for this book are rendered in tempera paint on
Manila paper.
Manufactured in China
0915 SCP
10 9 8 7 6 5 4 3 2
CIP data for this book is available from the Library of Congress.
ISBN 978-1-4814-0292-7
ISBN 978-1-4814-0293-4 (eBook)

Is mommy tall . . .

or short?

Sho

Is mommy pretty . . .

or ugly?

Is mommy nice . . .

or mean?

Me

Is mommy fun . . .

or boring?

ing!

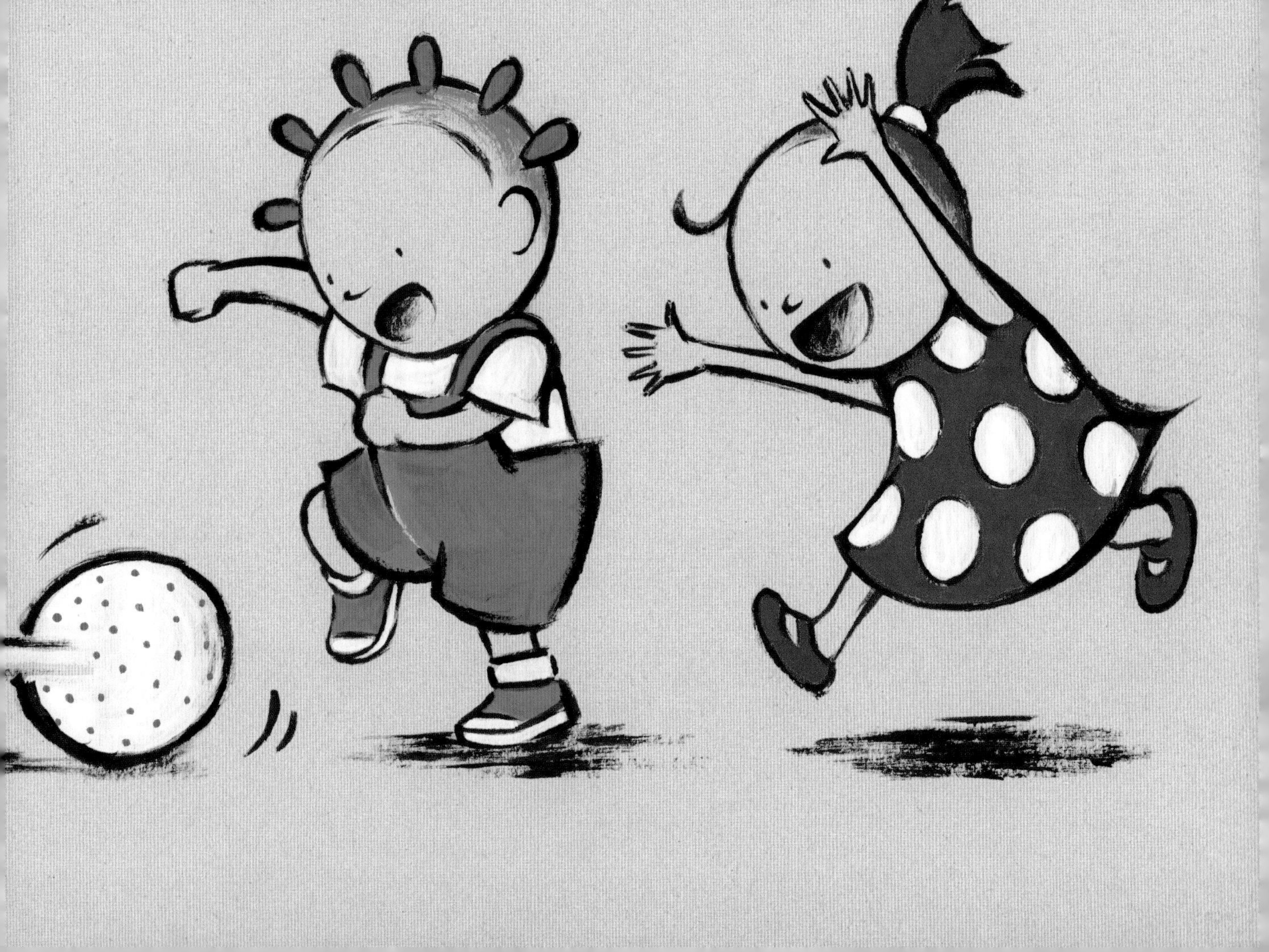

Is mommy young . . .

or old?

Is mommy neat . . .

or messy?

Do you love your short, ugly, mean

boring, old, messy mommy?